for Matan and Mümchen

The Word Collector

Text and illustrations © 2011 Sonja Wimmer
This edition © 2011 Cuento de Luz SL
Calle Claveles 10 | Urb Monteclaro | Pozuelo de Alarcón | 28223 Madrid | Spain | www.cuentodeluz.com
Original title in Spanish: La coleccionista de palabras
English translation by Jon Brokenbrow
Fourth printing
ISBN: 978-84-15241-34-8
Printed by Shanghai Chenxi Printing Co., Ltd. in PRC, August 2015, print number 1532-1

FSC
www.fsc.org
MIX
Paper from
responsible sources
FSC® C007923

CUENTO
DE LUZ

The WORD COLLECTOR

Sonja Wimmer

Luna was an extraordinary little girl. She lived **high, high,** high up in the **sky.**

words friendly funny Luna collected words just WORDS that words so BEAUTIFUL TICKLE your palate wi

that embrace your soul.

THAT they make you cry,

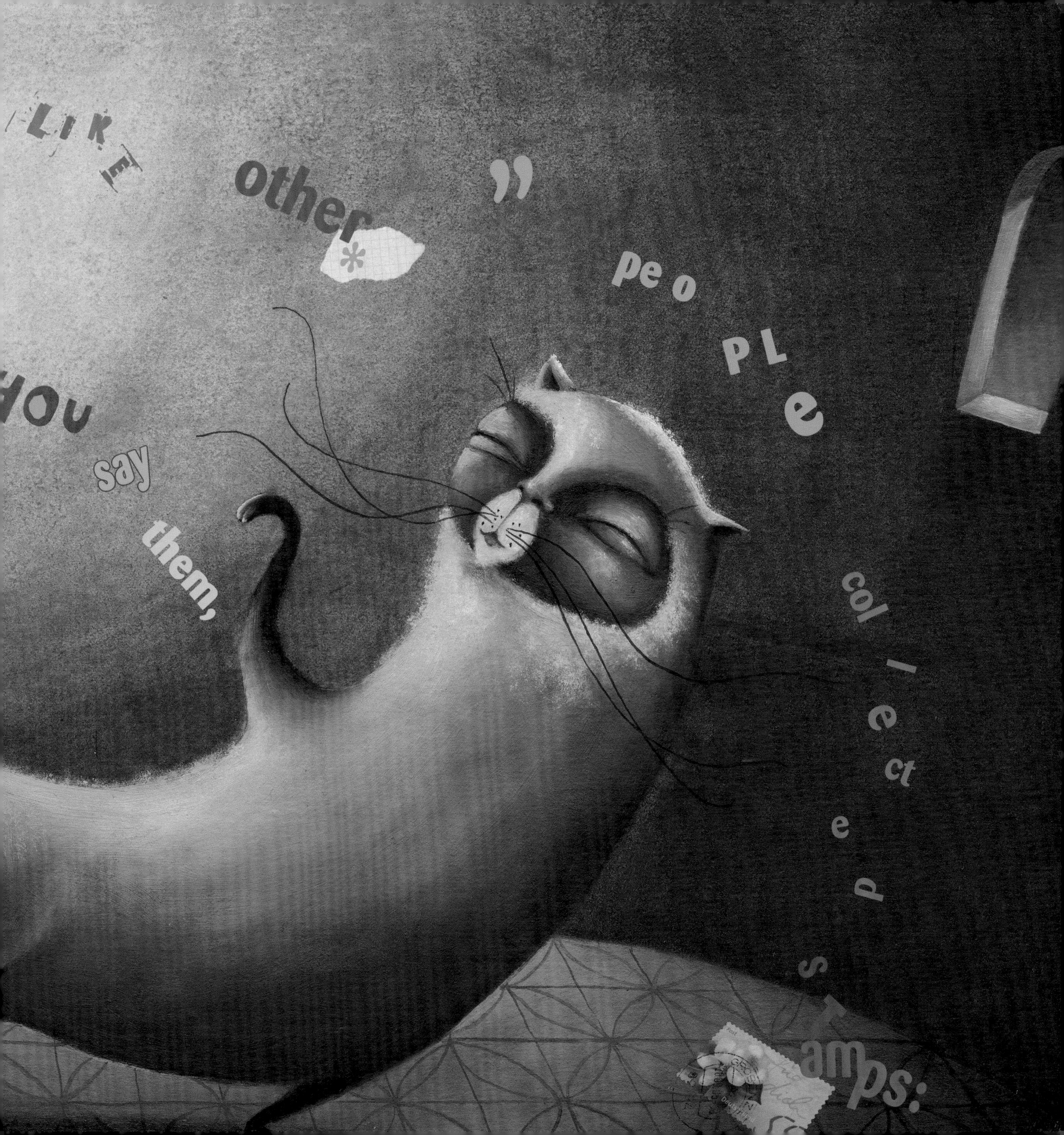
LIKE
other
”
peo PLe
you
say
them,
col l e ct e d
stamps:

But one day, everything changed.

Little, by little, the bEAutiful, magnificent AND words began to disappear.

Luna asked the **birds,** **the clouds** and the travelers

And they all replied

"People ar[...] the beautifu[...]

"The[...] they're imp[...]

"They're **too** [...]

...ame thing:

...orgetting all

...words."

...on't think

...ant any more."

...sy."

THAT NIGHT,
LUNA COULDN'T SLEEP.
AND WHEN THE FIRST RAYS OF SUNLIGHT
SENT THE STARS OFF TO BED,
SHE MADE A DECISION...

She had

into a big suitcase

and

them on a

journey.

She flew over seas and mountains an

Wherever there was hate and violence, she sowed words of brotherhood, love and tolerance within people's hearts.

Wherever there were people who were sad and lonely

she wove threads of warm words of friendship and compassion.

And where everyone was too busy to laugh together,
blind to the miracle of nature, she scattered the craziest, funnies
And the words tickled them in their noses, on their tongues and in the

...nd most magical words she had.

...ars.

But...

OH NO!

Suddenly, the suitcase was **empty**.

There wasn't a single **word** left!

Luna was **desperate.**

But then she saw that people had started to throw letters

They invented new words,

They gave them to each other, they shared them and they let them fly away again. to each other like balls.

And so, Luna sighed deeply and began to dance joyfully among them, together with her new friends. She had g

en them all of her words, but she was happy.

after all, what was the point of collecting something if you couldn't share it?

Page spread 1:

Luna was an extraordinary little girl. She lived high, high up in the sky.

Page spread 2:

And she had a very strange pastime.

Page spread 3:

Luna collected words just like other people collected stamps:
funny words, that tickle your palate when you say them,
words so beautiful that they make you cry,
friendly words that embrace your soul.

Page spread 4:

Magic words, delicious words, long and short words, funny words,
crazy words, magnificent words, little words, humble words, serious words ...

Page spread 5:

But one day, everything changed.
Little by little, the beautiful, magnificent and fun words began to disappear.
What had happened to them?

Page spread 6:

Luna asked the birds, the clouds and the travelers.
And they all replied the same thing:
"People are forgetting all the beautiful words.
They don't think they're important any more.
They're too busy."

Page spread 7:

That night, Luna couldn't sleep,
and when the first rays of sunlight sent the stars off to bed,
she made a decision.

Page spread 8:
She put all of the words she had in a big suitcase, and set off with them on a journey.

Page spread 9:
She flew over seas and continents, mountains and cities.

Page spread 10:
Wherever there was hate and violence, she sowed words
of brotherhood, love and tolerance within people's hearts.

Page spread 11:
Wherever there were people who were sad and lonely,
she wove threads of warm words, words of friendship and compassion.

Page spread 12:
And where everyone was too busy to laugh together, blind to the miracle of nature,
she scattered the craziest, funniest and most magical words she had.
And the words tickled them in their noses, on their tongues and in their ears.

Page spread 13:
But… Oh no! Suddenly, the suitcase was empty.
There wasn't a single word left! Luna was desperate.

Page spread 14:
But then she saw that people had started to throw letters to each other like balls.
They invented new words, they gave them to each other, they shared them,
and they let them fly away again.

Page spread 15:
And so, Luna sighed deeply and began to dance joyfully among them,
together with her new friends. She had given them all of her words, but she was happy.
After all, what was the point of collecting something if you couldn't share it?

ose de
tty. El Sup
página aducienc
está reñido co

Moderato.

Luna

Lächeln!